# KOALAS IN CAPES

## THE ZOMBIE CHICKENS

# KOALAS IN CAPES

## THE ZOMBIE CHICKENS

TERRIE CHILVERS

ILLUSTRATED BY

DAVID O'CONNELL

nosy crow

First published in the UK in 2026 by Nosy Crow Ltd
Wheat Wharf, 27a Shad Thames,
London, SE1 2XZ, UK

Nosy Crow Eireann Ltd
c/o Fieldfisher Ireland LLP
45 Mespil Road,
Dublin 4, D04 W2F1, Ireland



ISBN: 978 1 80513 220 2

A CIP catalogue record for this book is available from the British Library.



Printed and bound in Great Britain by Clays Ltd, Elcograf S.p.A. following rigorous ethical sourcing standards.

FSC www.fsc.org
MIX
Paper | Supporting responsible forestry
FSC® C018072

1 3 5 7 9 10 8 6 4 2

www.nosycrow.com

For Harriet
T.C.

To Becky
D.O.

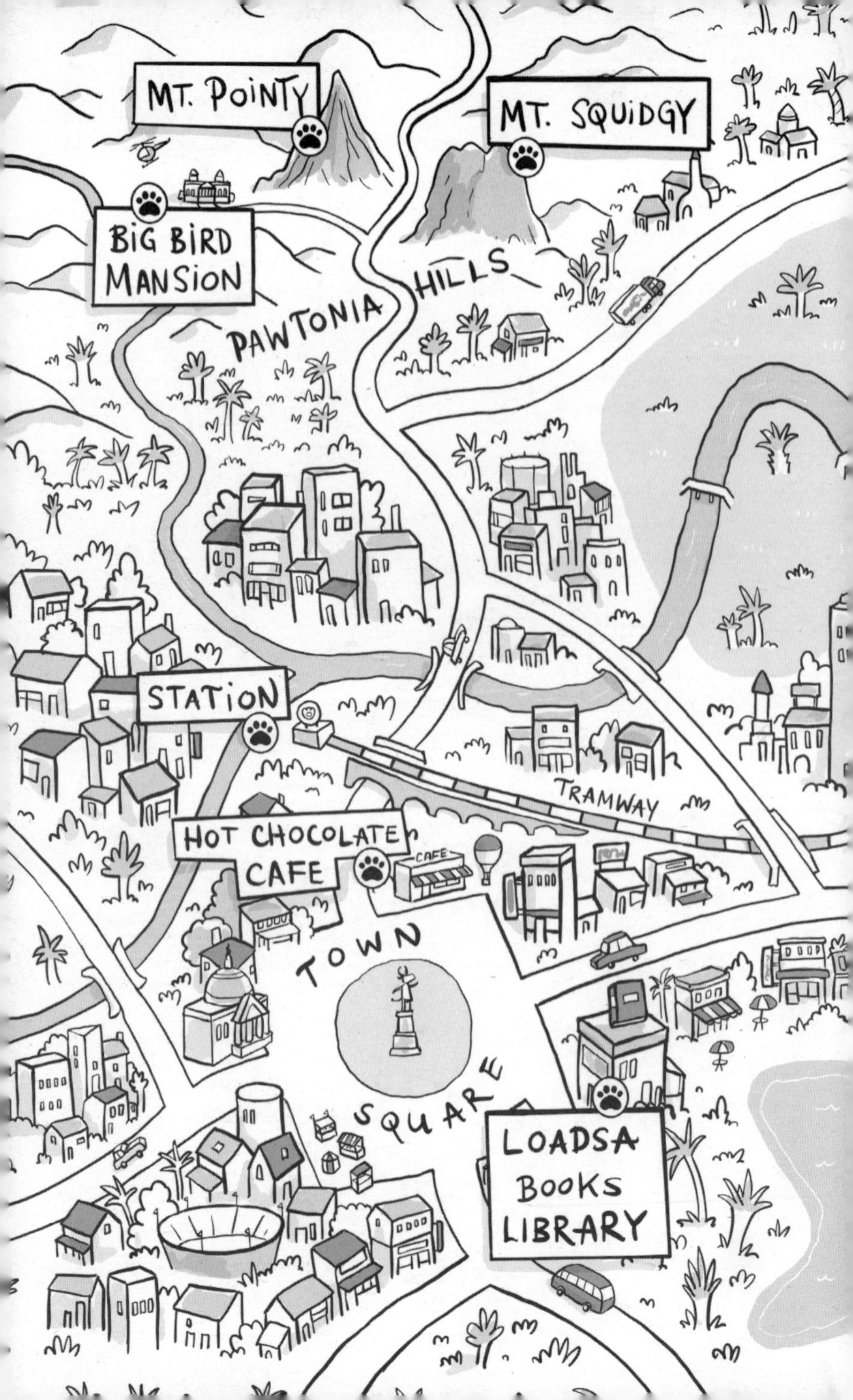
MT. POINTY
MT. SQUIDGY
BIG BIRD MANSION
PAWTONIA HILLS
STATION
TRAMWAY
HOT CHOCOLATE CAFE
CAFE
TOWN SQUARE
LOADSA BOOKS LIBRARY

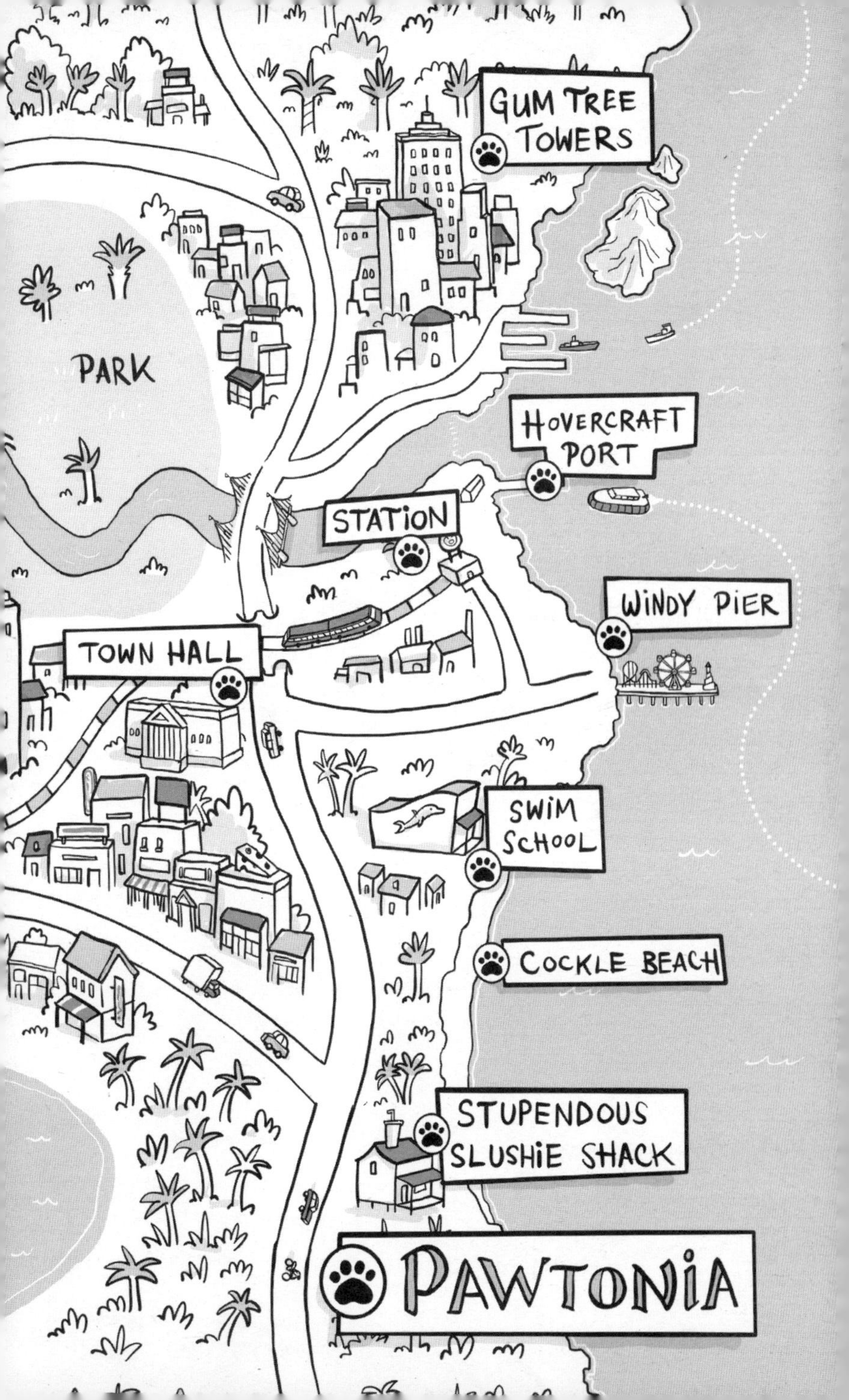
GUM TREE TOWERS
PARK
HOVERCRAFT PORT
STATION
WINDY PIER
TOWN HALL
SWIM SCHOOL
COCKLE BEACH
STUPENDOUS SLUSHIE SHACK
PAWTONIA

# PROLOGUE

**A GIANT OSTRICH** smashed open an old wooden box and pulled out a very dusty scroll. It was tied with a red ribbon and had a label that said:

**SECRET LEGEND (AUTHORISED READERS ONLY).**

The ostrich quickly unrolled the scroll and read:

## SECRET LEGEND #367

**On the Ninth day of the Ninth month there will be a Day of Darkness when the Sun is driven from the sky and all of Pawtonia is plunged into deepest night! On this very day, two infant koalas, sleeping soundly in their cribs, shall have great powers bestowed upon them.**

**The koalas' powers will emerge on their ninth birthday and they will join forces to create the best**

SECRET SUPERPOWERED KOALA DUO

**the world has ever seen. Aided by a long-snouted young genius, they will fight to save Pawtonia from all things evil, nasty and downright horrible.**

The giant ostrich fluffed out his wings and snorted angrily. He'd always hated koalas.

# CHAPTER 1

## Somewhere on a Rooftop in Pawtonia

"**KOALAS, ASSEMBLE!**" said Bob the koala, as he stood on the rooftop of his apartment block, Gum Tree Towers.

But Archie, his best koala friend, was nowhere to be seen. Bob tucked his superhero leggings into his superhero boots and practised his superhero pose. He

placed his paws on his furry hips and looked into the distance as though he'd just saved a family of cats from a burning building using his super strength. Bob and Archie had only had their superhero powers for a few weeks, but Bob was already loving it.

"Archie?" called Bob.

"Coming!" shouted Archie. Bob turned round but there was no sign of his friend, just a rucksack suspended in the air, bobbing towards him.

"Archie, you're in invisible mode," said Bob.

"Oh, sorry, I was practising," said Archie as he appeared in front of Bob. "Managed to stay invisible for twenty seconds! That's the longest time so far!"

"Well done! But where were you? I did the 'koalas, assemble' call ages ago," said Bob.

"Sorry about that," replied Archie. "My cape got stuck in the door."

"No problem," said Bob. "You're here now, and the

SUPER KOALA SQUAD

is ready for action!"

"Can we call ourselves a squad when there's only two of us?" said Archie. "What about

THE MAGNIFICENT MARSUPIALS OF PAWTONIA?"

"It's a bit of a mouthful," said Bob. "Wait,

I've got it!

KOALAS IN CAPES!"

"Well, I guess if we must have a name, that's the best one," said Archie. "But are we ready for a proper mission? We only learned how to fly last week, and look what happened when we tried to rescue that baby goat from up a tree."

Bob readjusted his cape. "This isn't the time for doubts. And that could have happened to anyone. We need to practise our superhero skills so we're ready to save

Pawtonia from the evil Dr Colossus!"

Everyone was talking about a giant ostrich called Dr Colossus, the

**SUPERVILLAIN**

behind a surge in criminal activity across the city. Bob was determined the Koalas in Capes would be the ones to catch him. It was their duty!

Bob and Archie looked out across Pawtonia. It was a super-sunny afternoon. The Hot Chocolate Café was buzzing with customers and there was a kangaroo steel drum band playing for a group of tourist otters in the city square.

"Everything seems totally fine!" said Archie, looking relieved. "Shall we just go and have a Triple Chocolate Humdinger at the Hot Chocolate Café?"

But then a sudden, shrill alarm rang out, and Archie's face fell.

"It's coming from the massive gift shop!" said Bob excitedly, peering through some binoculars that he'd grabbed from Archie's rucksack.

"What massive gift shop? Pawtonia doesn't have a massive gift shop," said

Archie, looking puzzled.

"Yes, it does! You know, the place with all the great pens and novelty mugs. Oh, and some dusty old stuff too," said Bob.

"You mean the Natural History Museum?" said Archie.

But Bob was too busy peering through the binoculars to answer. "There's a ginormous traffic jam on Eucalyptus Road – it will take the police ages to get there! Come on. We need to get going!"

Archie was pacing around, looking concerned. "But don't we need a plan?"

"We've got one," said Bob. "We fly over

there and stop the robbery! With my

SUPER STRENGTH

and your

POWER OF INVISIBILITY

we're unstoppable. Being superheroes is in our blood."

"Thing is, Bob, I'm not sure it is in my blood," said Archie. "A few weeks ago I was just a regular koala and I really liked it that way. Then suddenly there's a freaky solar eclipse and now I can turn invisible. It's all very weird."

But Bob was already hovering in the air next to Archie. "You'll be great, I promise. And anyway, Pawtonia needs us."

"All right, all right," said Archie. "But I'm not doing any scary stuff..."

A moment later, there were two young koalas in the skies above Pawtonia. Bob soared through the air like a furry torpedo. His cape fluttered in the wind behind him and he felt supersonic! Bob glanced back to make sure Archie was keeping up.

Archie was bobbing around in the sky like a plane with a dodgy engine.

"Can we take the bus next time?" shouted Archie. "Flying makes me travel sick."

But Bob had a faraway look on his face

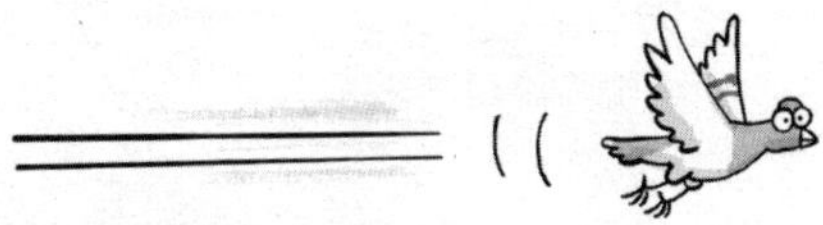

and didn't answer.

"Bob, are you listening?" said Archie, his furry face turning a bit green.

"Yes, I'm totally listening," said Bob, who totally wasn't listening. He was daydreaming about how they'd soon be saving the world, not just Pawtonia. They were going to be legends! They might even get a sponsorship deal from the city and buy swankier capes.

"Look, we're almost there!" said Bob excitedly, as he spotted the museum just across the river. Koalas in Capes were on their first proper mission!

# CHAPTER 2

## Meanwhile, at the Museum...

**DR COLOSSUS** peered at a bank of computer screens from the comfort of Big Bird Mansion in the Pawtonia Hills. He had a meerkat working undercover at the Natural History Museum who had hacked the security cameras. And now Dr Colossus had a beady eye on every inch of the museum.

The museum was closed for the evening, which made it perfect for a heist!

Dr Colossus smiled to himself as he watched the robber ducks enter the

**CURSED ARTEFACTS DEPARTMENT.**

They were carrying swag bags and shining torches on the display cabinets as they searched for something VERY important.

"There it is!" shouted Dr Colossus, watching the screens. "The mummified chicken! Grab it!"

The robber ducks smashed the glass case containing the prized artefact. Mandy, the

head robber duck, quickly shoved it in a large swag bag. A few seconds later, the museum's alarm went off and a group of security sheep appeared. But Dr Colossus wasn't worried – the robber ducks were prepared...

"Deploy the pondweed whumpers!" he shouted into his headset.

One of the robber ducks threw a whumper into the path of the sheep.

BOOM!
SPLUUURGGE!!

It exploded into a swampy puddle of pondweed and soon the security sheep were tangled in its slimy tendrils. The robber ducks could make their escape!

Back at Big Bird Mansion, Dr Colossus watched with glee and clapped his huge feathery wings. He loved it when a plan came together. Now that they had the mummified chicken, he was one step closer to taking full control of the city.

Dr Colossus had been a bit worried by the legend of the superhero koalas, but so far he'd only heard about two amateurs who had tried to rescue a baby goat that didn't

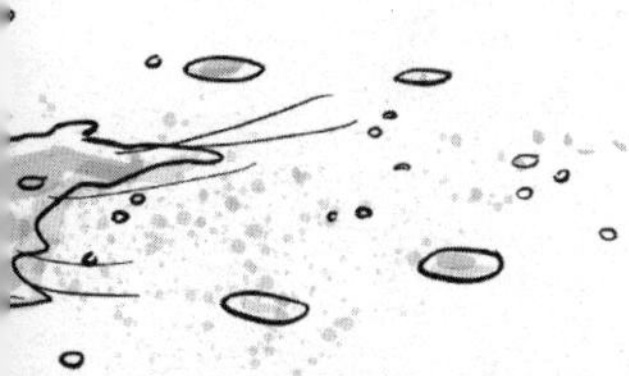

need rescuing. And they REALLY didn't seem like anything to worry about.

Then something caught his eye. A robber duck had broken away from the escaping group and was in the

SHINY JEWELS DEPARTMENT

scooping gold jewellery into a sack.

"Zelda!" shouted Dr Colossus. "Get out of there! That's not part of the mission!"

Dr Colossus sighed. Robber ducks will be robber ducks...

# ★ CHAPTER 3 ★

## Robber Ducks

**BOB AND ARCHIE** landed on the roof of a cinema close to the museum. Well, Bob landed and Archie stumbled around and then fell over.

"This is ridiculous, Bob. I can't be a superhero," said Archie, panicking. "I can't fly without feeling sick and I can't even land without falling over. How am I supposed to fight crime?"

Bob put a paw on his shoulder. "Archie, you can turn invisible; that's

TOTALLY COOL.

Even cooler than my super strength. Although that's pretty cool too. And anyway, we're a team, so you can just be on the roof keeping watch if you like. I'll do all the superheroey stuff."

Archie nodded.

"Can you check out the area?" asked Bob.

"You're better at that sort of thing."

Archie got out his binoculars and panned around the museum. This calmed him down – he was always less stressed when he had a task to do.

"There are three ducks in balaclavas exiting the back of the museum," said Archie. "They've got swag bags and pondweed whumpers!"

Bob nodded. He'd heard about pondweed whumpers – if one exploded in your path, it was like wading through treacle. These robber ducks weren't messing about.

"Look!" he said, peering at a big black car

parked on the road beneath them. "That must be the getaway car. It's got blacked-out windows. I need to move fast!"

"Bob, wait!" said Archie. "You don't know for sure that's—"

But Bob was already flying towards the car. He hovered in mid-air and grabbed hold of the bonnet. Then he lifted up the car as if it were made of feathers. Bob felt a warm glow inside. This mission was going really well! He looked down and noticed three ducks in balaclavas heading towards him.

"Let's get out of here," shouted one of the ducks to her crew. "In the car, quick!"

Bob chuckled to himself. There was no car for them to jump in and the kangatroopers were on their way! Bob spun the getaway car on his finger like a basketball – having super strength was great!

But then Bob watched as, strangely, the ducks walked right past him, got into their

**BRIGHT-RED GETAWAY CAR**

and started to drive away!

Bob's face fell. If that was the robbers' car, whose car was he holding above his head? Out of the corner of his eye, Bob could see

Archie on the cinema rooftop, waving his arms around frantically.

Bob watched as the driver's window opened and an angry bushbaby chauffeur stuck his head out.

"Hey!" he said. "What's going on?"

"Erm, there's been a bit of a misunderstanding," said Bob.

The bushbaby looked down and suddenly realised his car was floating in mid-air. "Help!" he yelled. "Someone help! I've been captured by a flying koala!"

Bob gulped. The robber ducks were getting away and he'd accidentally kidnapped a bushbaby. Being a superhero wasn't as easy as it looked!

# CHAPTER 4

## The Kangatroopers

**BOB FLEW DOWN** and placed the bushbaby and his car carefully on the ground.

"What on earth did you think you were doing?" said the bushbaby, scrambling out of his car, looking very angry.

Bob put his paws on his furry hips as his

cape fluttered in the wind. He was trying to explain when a crisp packet blew into his face. He swatted it away and tried again.

Meanwhile, Archie had flown down from the rooftop.

"We'd love to stop and talk," said Archie, "but I'm afraid we have to stop a robbery!"

And the two Koalas in Capes quickly hurried away from the angry bushbaby.

"I knew we should have made a plan!" said Archie, giving Bob the side-eye. "I overheard some of the security guard sheep saying a mummified chicken has been stolen. Most of the robber ducks have already got away but I spotted one still hanging around at the back of the museum. They must have accidentally left her behind."

"Then that's where we need to be!" said Bob. "Let's go!"

But as Bob and Archie turned to run towards the museum, they crashed straight into a duck carrying a large sack.

"Oh, excuse me," quacked the robber duck. "I was just on my way to the – the—"

"The getaway car?" said Archie. "With your loot?"

"What, this?" said the duck, jangling the sack. "Oh, this is just my handbag. It's

the new Ducky Loot Satchel. All the most stylish poultry have them!"

"A likely story!" said Bob, as two police motorbikes screeched round the corner with a police van following close behind, siren blaring. Two kangatroopers bounced off their bikes and approached Bob, Archie and the robber duck. And a separate band of kangatroopers bounced off in the direction of the museum.

The duck tried to make a run for it, but her swag bag made it more of a fast waddle. Bob dived towards her as she abandoned the sack and started to fly off, but her webbed feet slipped through his paws.

Quick as a flash, one of the kangatroopers jumped into the air ...

**BOIIIINNNGGG**

... grabbed the duck mid-flight, popped her safely in her pouch and thumped back down on to the pavement again.

The other kangatrooper went to retrieve the swag bag. "I'm Detective Steel," she said to Bob and Archie. "Who are you?" She

looked suspiciously at their capes.

"We're Koalas in Capes!" said Bob proudly. "Here to protect Pawtonia from all things mean and dangerous!"

Bob and Archie went to strike their special superhero pose with their backs to each other and arms folded. Except Archie was a bit too far away and they both ended up falling backwards on their bums.

The kangatrooper with the robber duck in her pouch bounced over. "Wait! I know you two! We had to deal with two very unhappy goats last week who thought you were trying to kidnap their daughter."

"That was a misunderstanding," said Archie.

"And we really think we can help this time!" said Bob. "It's our duty to the citizens of Pawtonia!"

"I think the citizens of Pawtonia will be much safer with you two off the streets!" said Detective Steel. "We believe this heist is the work of the very dangerous supervillain ostrich, Dr Colossus. Who knows what he wants with a

MUMMIFIED CHICKEN

but we're going to find out!"

Bob's eyes widened. He hadn't expected to cross paths with Dr Colossus quite so soon.

Archie looked like he might throw up.

"So we'll take it from here," said Detective Steel. "We've been on Dr Colossus's feathery tail for ages – the last thing we need is two koalas messing things up."

And with that, the two kangatroopers bundled the robber duck into the back of the police van. As they did so, a small rectangular piece of card fell from the duck's pocket. Bob quickly picked it up before the kangatroopers could see it.

"Look!" he whispered, handing the card to Archie. "It's an invitation to a supervillains' ball at Big Bird Mansion up in the Pawtonia Hills. That must be where all the robber ducks are heading. If we go to the ball, we'll find Dr Colossus AND the mummified chicken!

WE'LL BE HEROES!"

"I don't know,' said Archie. "Why don't we

just give the invite to the kangatroopers and leave it to the professionals? We could go and get a nice, safe hot chocolate."

Bob shook his furry head. "The kangatroopers might be decent at catching ordinary criminals, but vanquishing a supervillain requires

**SUPERHERO SKILLS."**

Archie watched as the police van drove away, along with their chance to hand over the invitation. "OK, fine, but we're definitely going to need Quinn's help on this one."

Quinn was Bob and Archie's best friend. She was an aardvark and the ONLY animal who knew the real identities of Koalas in Capes. She was a

SCIENCE WHIZZ

who made amazing gadgets, and she'd promised to invent some to help them fight crime.

Oh, and her mum happened to run the best hot chocolate café in all of Pawtonia...

# ★ CHAPTER 5 ★

## The Hot Chocolate Café

**BOB AND ARCHIE** changed out of their superhero outfits and walked down Ash Avenue. Instead of the usual steady stream of customers and the specials board outside the Hot Chocolate Café, there was an enormous hot-air balloon blocking the entire street. Cars were honking and pedestrians were trying to squeeze round the balloon's basket.

"What's that doing there?" said Archie.

Outside the café, Quinn's mum was angrily talking to a zebra with a clipboard and sniffing at the hot-air balloon with her long snout.

"I did not order this!" she said. "You'll just have to take it back!"

Quinn's mum was smaller than the average aardvark but she knew how to make herself heard.

"Hello there, boys!" she said, spotting Bob and Archie. "I'm just dealing with a bit of bother! This balloon was supposed to fly around the city and advertise the café. But there was a mix-up at BIG BALLOONZ R US."

Bob and Archie read the words on the side of the balloon:

**THE HOT CHOCOLATE CAFÉ MAKES THE BEST HOT STINKS IN TOWN!**

Bob and Archie tried not to giggle.

"I'm afraid that's what you asked for," said the zebra.

CAFE
CHOCOLATE
10

"No, we didn't!" said Quinn's mum. "It should be hot drinks! DRINKS!"

"Well, I'm afraid you signed the paperwork yesterday, Mrs Burrows, so this hot-air balloon is yours for forty-eight hours."

Quinn's mum sighed. "Well, at least put it round the back in the car park. You're blocking the whole street and nobody can see the specials board."

Bob and Archie pushed open the door of the Hot Chocolate Café. The bell tinkled and the warm scent of chocolate and toasted marshmallows filled their nostrils.

"Can I interest you in a Quadruple

Chocoloco-lyptus Explosion?" said Quinn's mum, grabbing her apron.

"Yes, please!" said Bob and Archie together.

Quinn's mum whipped up the drinks super quickly. "Quinn's doing a stocktake of the marshmallows out the back. Take a hot chocolate for her too."

"Thanks, Mrs Burrows!" said Archie, grabbing the drinks as they made their way through to the marshmallow storeroom at the back of the café.

It was where Quinn did all of her inventing.

"EUCALYPTUS!" shouted Archie through the keyhole.

Quinn opened the door as soon as she heard the password. She was wearing her favourite pair of purple safety goggles and a white lab coat.

"Oh, hi, guys," she said, heading back to her workbench. It was covered with tools, test tubes, and all kinds of strange-looking contraptions. The surrounding marshmallow boxes provided excellent soundproofing for her sawing and hammering, but it was especially useful now that the cupboard had to double as a

TOP-SECRET SUPERHERO HQ.

"We need your help, Quinn," said Archie. "Dr Colossus is up to something!"

"The kangatroopers think he was behind a robbery at the museum today," Bob explained. "An ancient mummified chicken was stolen."

"What does he want an ancient mummified chicken for?" said Quinn.

"Whatever he wants it for, we need to stop him. One of his robber ducks dropped this," said Bob, handing over the invitation.

"You were there?" said Quinn, wide-eyed, her long ears pricking up even more than usual.

"Yep!" said Bob. "And this invite could lead us to Dr Colossus."

"Can I just say, I really don't think it's a good idea to go," said Archie. "It's a

SUPERVILLAINS' BALL!

It could be

REALLY DANGEROUS.

And what exactly would we do when we got there?"

Bob's eyes shone. "Find the mummified

chicken, prove that Dr Colossus was responsible for stealing it, then get him locked up in prison where he belongs! We'll be total heroes."

"But we haven't even dealt with ONE supervillain yet! What happens when there's a whole mega cluster of them?" said Archie.

A smile spread across Quinn's face. "I might have something to help with that..."

# CHAPTER 6

## The Boogie Blaster

"**THIS IS TOTALLY** a mission that Koalas in Capes can handle," said Quinn. "You just need the right tools for the job!"

She picked up a shiny new gadget from her workbench. It looked like a mini super soaker.

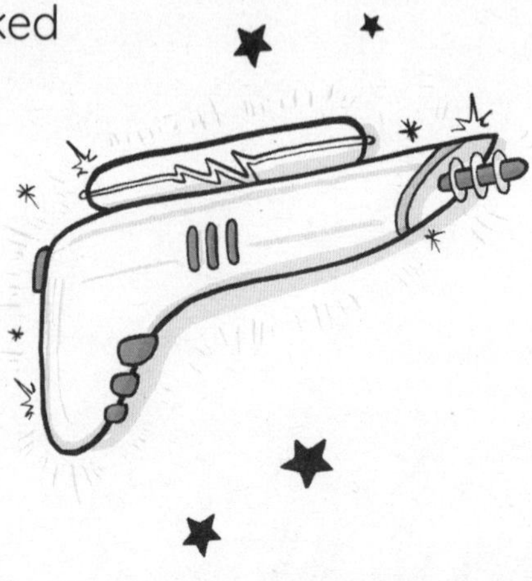

"Meet ...

the

**BOOGIE BLASTER!"**

she said with an excited flourish. "One blast and your villain will be dancing all the way to the police station!"

Bob's face lit up. "And it definitely works?"

"Yep, well, I've only tested it on bugs so far," said Quinn. "It just needs a quick test on a larger animal and it's good to go."

Bob and Quinn turned to Archie.

"What? Why me?" said Archie.

"The boogie blaster won't harm you," said Quinn. "Your fur might turn bright green, that's all. But I'm pretty certain I've fixed that."

Archie gulped.

"You always say that testing things is really important," said Bob.

"Not when it involves me breakdancing in a very tight space or turning green for experimental purposes!" said Archie.

"Fine, I'll do it," said Bob. "How long will it make me dance for?"

"Only about five minutes," said Quinn, as she pointed the blaster at Bob and flicked a switch. "But there's no way of knowing which dance you'll do."

The boogie blaster started whirring like a washing machine as it powered up. Quinn hit the trigger and a bright-red laser beam shot out and lit up Bob like a Christmas tree.

"Are you OK?" said Archie.

"Totally fine," said Bob. "Didn't feel a thing. But I do have a very strong urge to ...

DO THE WORM!"

And within seconds, Bob was breakdancing around the room uncontrollably.

“OK, safe to say it works just fine,” said Quinn, grabbing the blaster excitedly with her claws. She handed it to Archie to put in his rucksack, as Bob did a rather impressive head spin.

"Now you can go to the supervillains' ball and protect yourselves if you get into any trouble," said Quinn. "And could you make a note of what dances the blaster makes the animals do? That would be really helpful for my research."

"But what will we tell our parents?" said Archie, looking nervous.

"Good point," said Bob, getting to his feet. "We need a cover story."

"Tell them our school project on Egyptian scarab beetles is proving particularly tricky and we're all working on it together at the library," said Quinn.

"FANTASTIC!" shouted Bob. He took a final swig of his hot chocolate and wiped away his froth moustache, then he stood up and put his paws on his furry hips. "It's time for Koalas in Capes to head to the

SUPERVILLAINS' BALL!"

# CHAPTER 7

## Secret Legend #74

**DR COLOSSUS** had been delighted with the ancient scrolls he'd obtained from a villainous dolphin. The one with the legend of two superhero koalas wasn't the most interesting, though...

## SECRET LEGEND #74

A plucky chicken preserved in bandages holds the power to unleash the undead. When its poultry brothers and sisters gaze upon its unwrapped form, they shall immediately transform into

ZOMBIE CHICKENS!

And now Dr Colossus had his wings on the exact plucky chicken he needed!

"Excellent job, robber ducks!" he said. "Now we must unwrap our feathered friend."

As Dr Colossus pulled back the bandages and blew away the dust, he revealed the ancient mummified chicken. Its eyes were glowing bright red.

"Gather the poultry," said Dr Colossus. "It's time to unleash ...

THE ZOMBIE

CHICKEN

APOCALYPSE!"

# CHAPTER 8

## The Supervillains' Ball

**BOB AND ARCHIE** flew over the Pawtonia Hills. It was the quickest way to get to the supervillains' ball, and the most fun too, thought Bob. Through the clouds they could see the tops of Mount Pointy and Mount Squidgy. From this high up, the houses dotted about looked like tiny pieces of Lego. Apart from one, which was much bigger than the rest, with lots of cars driving towards it like tiny ants.

"That must be Big Bird Mansion!" said Bob.

Bob and Archie landed at the start of the long gravel driveway that led to the mansion. They were wearing their very best tuxedos from the time they'd done koala-oke. Bob was holding the invitation in his paws and Archie was tightly gripping the straps of his rucksack. Inside was the boogie blaster and a thermos of hot chocolate for emergencies.

Two tough-looking armadillo bouncers were ushering a group of well-dressed wombats inside the mansion. And just ahead of Bob and Archie was a giraffe in a velvet suit surrounded by a gaggle of geese in sequined ball gowns. The geese were fanning themselves and taking selfies.

"What if they check our bags?" whispered Archie. "I've got the boogie blaster in here!"

"It's a supervillains' ball," replied Bob. "They'd probably throw us out if we DIDN'T have any weapons!"

Archie looked even more nervous as they approached the door. "Then maybe we should have more weapons. Is it too late to go back and get some?"

"We'll be fine," said Bob. "Just try to look chill."

Archie smiled so tightly it looked like he needed the toilet.

"Name!" said the first armadillo in a very aggressive tone, which Bob felt was unnecessary. Just because they were in the business of supervillainy, didn't mean they had to be rude.

"Erm, we're not on the list," said Bob. "We're keeping a low profile. But we've got an invite."

"No problem, sirs," said the armadillo, taking the invitation and nodding his head.

The plates of armour on his back clanged as he stepped back.

Bob nudged Archie and gave him a little wink. They were almost in. These guys didn't suspect a thing!

"But of course we will need the

**SECRET HANDSHAKE,"**

said the armadillo, blocking their path.

Bob's smile faded. "Erm, of course. I'm a bit rusty but..."

Bob grabbed the armadillo's claw and shook it around before ending in what looked like a cross between a high five and jazz hands.

"I've added a few extra bits," said Bob. "But that should give you the gist."

Bob held his breath. He was sure he could hear Archie's knees knocking.

The armadillo grinned. "Nice try, but all good supervillains know that we don't do secret handshakes..."

He turned to the second armadillo. "So what should we do with these chumps? Should we report them to the boss?"

"Not worth wasting his time," said the second armadillo.

"We could always feed them to the

ZOMBIE CHICKENS,"

chuckled the first armadillo.

The second armadillo shoved him. "We're not supposed to mention the zombie chickens!"

"Oh right, I forgot!" said the first armadillo. He turned to Bob and Archie. "Go on, scram. Leave the property immediately or we'll set the robot guard dogs on you."

Bob and Archie hurried back down the gravel driveway.

"Well, that went brilliantly to plan and wasn't at all terrifying," said Archie.

"I've got another idea," said Bob, already on the case.

"I don't want to know," said Archie. "You heard what the armadillos said about setting robot dogs on us. And what was that about zombie chickens?! Do you think it's something to do with the mummified chicken they stole?"

But Bob was watching a group of gazelles in waiter outfits as they strode past the main entrance and walked round the side.

"There's another entrance, Archie!" said Bob. "You just need to turn invisible and follow someone in. Then nab us some waiters' jackets and we can walk straight in."

Archie looked horrified. “I can’t go in by myself! What if my invisibility wears off while I’m inside!”

“We’re superheroes, Archie,” said Bob, puffing out his chest. “It’s our duty to save the animals of Pawtonia!”

“I guess you’re right,” said Archie. “I’ll just have to be a very nervous superhero.”

“Totally fine!” said Bob, and the plan was underway.

# CHAPTER 9

## Very Important Big Bird Activity

**DR COLOSSUS** was watching CCTV screens showing footage from around the mansion. He swivelled round in a big swivelly chair to face the robber ducks.

"It's time for the next phase of my master plan!"

"What's that, boss?" said Mandy, the leader

of the ducks, who had a tiara on her head and an Ancient Egyptian diamond anklet around her neck. All of the other ducks were also jangling with jewels.

"What on earth are you all wearing?" said Dr Colossus.

"Just the spoils from the museum mission," said Mandy.

"Well, can you tone it down a bit? The mission isn't over yet," said Dr Colossus. "And we don't want any kangatroopers seeing you walking around in museum bling."

The robber ducks looked a bit shifty

and quietly took off their necklaces and bangles.

"Tonight's the night of the Supervillains' Ball here at Big Bird Mansion," said Dr Colossus. "Except we all know what's really happening!"

"What's that, boss?" said Mandy, surrounded by a group of blank-looking ducks.

Dr Colossus sighed. Working with robber ducks was infuriating sometimes. "It's the night I finally take control of Pawtonia!" he boomed.

Mandy and the robber ducks still looked

blank. Some of them were handing round a bag of earthworms.

"You know, the zombie chickens?" said Dr Colossus.

"How does that work then, boss?" asked Mandy, between mouthfuls.

"I'm going to threaten Pawtonia with my army of zombie chickens! They'll have to do whatever I say, unless they want undead poultry let loose across the city. And that means making me Mayor!"

"And what do we have to do, boss?" said Mandy.

"It's very simple," said Dr Colossus. "You

just need to keep an eye on the security cameras and let me know immediately if you see any kangatroopers ...

or those

PESKY KOALAS!"

"Got it, boss!" said Mandy, and the rest of the robber ducks nodded in agreement while sharing the bag of crispy earthworms.

"And meanwhile I'll be broadcasting a

VERY SPECIAL AND
VERY EVIL MESSAGE

to the whole of the city. If they don't make me the Mayor of Pawtonia, I'll release my zombie chicken army on the city! One peck and they'll all be zombie-fied!"

Dr Colossus threw his head back and let out an evil laugh. He flapped his wings so excitedly that he knocked over Mandy's salmon slushie.

"MWAHAHAHAHAHAHAHHA!
MWAHAHAHAHAHAHAHHAHAHAHAHAHAH!"

"Would you like an earthworm, boss?" said one of the ducks.

"Ooh, yes, please," said Dr Colossus. "And then I have a ball to host!"

# CHAPTER 10

## Peck Peck Squawk

"Psssst!" said Archie. He waved at Bob as he emerged from the side entrance wearing a waiter's jacket. "The coast is clear!"

"Well done! I knew you could do it!" said Bob, putting on the second jacket.

"I think my powers are getting stronger," said Archie, looking almost surprised at himself and possibly even a tiny bit excited. "I managed to stay invisible for five seconds longer than usual!"

"Great. Now, let's get back in there!" said Bob, leading the way.

"Once we get further inside, there are loads of catering staff," whispered Archie, "so we'll have to find the artefact as quickly as possible so nobody notices us."

"Spoken like a true superhero!" said Bob loudly.

"Shh," said Archie. "They might hear you!"

Nearby, there were lots of waiters who were ducking in and out of a busy kitchen with trays of food.

"Now, stay close and don't make eye contact with anyone," said Bob.

They weaved their way through the staff, looking for a clue as to where the mummified chicken might be. Two waiters holding trays piled high with canapés set off deeper into the mansion, and Bob and Archie decided to follow them. They headed down another long corridor with a plush red carpet and paintings of supervillains on the walls.

At the end, the waiters pushed open a door. Inside there was a huge ballroom full of animals milling around with cocktails and canapés.

Creatures of all shapes and sizes were decked out in feather boas, bow ties and sequins. Bob caught a glimpse of a crocodile in a tuxedo with diamond-encrusted teeth gleaming under the lights of a glittering chandelier.

"Best avoid going in there," said Archie with a nervous laugh as they quickly retreated.

Bob scratched his furry chin. "Now, if we were a giant supervillain ostrich, where would we hide a mummified chicken?"

Just then a voice boomed, "I need two waiters! Anyone without a tray, I've got a job for you!"

Bob and Archie jumped head first into a rack of coats. They waited quietly until it felt safe enough to peek out. They saw two possum waiters being handed huge trays of mini trifles to carry into the ballroom.

"Phew, that was close," said Bob.

As they emerged from the coat rack, Bob spotted something at the other end of the corridor. It was in a dark area where none of the waiting staff were going.

"Archie, let's look over there!" said Bob as they hurried down the corridor. At the end was a door with a sign that said:

**BASEMENT - DO NOT ENTER.**

"The mummified chicken must be in here!" said Bob, with his paw already on the door handle.

"Wait! I'm not sure about this, Bob," said

Archie. “Maybe we should look in some other less creepy places?”

“Are you kidding? Come on! The important stuff is always in the basement!” said Bob.

“No, it’s not!” said Archie. “The SCARY stuff is always in the basement!”

But Bob had already opened the door and was slowly creeping down the steps.

There was a flickering light bulb at the top of the stairs. It gave off just enough light for the two koalas to see the next step in front of them.

“Come on,” said Bob. “If we can find the stolen artefact we can prove that

Dr Colossus is responsible and get him locked up in prison where he belongs!"

"OK," said Archie. "But can you stop making that pecking noise. It's a bit annoying."

"What pecking noise?" said Bob.

PECK PECK

"That's not me," said Bob. "Are you sure it isn't you?"

"No! I think I'd know if I was making a pecking noise!" whispered Archie.

PECK PECK PECK

PECK!

PECK!

PECK!

"What on earth is that!" said Bob, finally reaching the bottom of the staircase and frantically feeling around on the wall. "It's so dark in here! There must be a light switch somewhere..."

At last he found the switch and quickly flicked it on. As light filled the room, Bob and Archie realised they were not alone.

# CHAPTER 11

## Pass the Boogie Blaster!

SQUAAAWWWKKK!

“I think we might have found the zombie chickens,” said Bob.

Five zombie chickens were staring directly at Bob and Archie. Their eyes were red and bulging and they looked like someone had blown them up and stuck them back together. Behind them was a chicken coop surrounded by wire fencing.

"I guess they chewed their way through," said Archie, seeing the big hole in the fencing.

"Maybe if we don't make any fast moves they'll leave us alone," said Bob.

But Archie had disappeared.

"I'm in invisible mode but you should hide," said Archie.

But one of the chickens was already looking at the top of Bob's head.

"BRAAINNNNSS!"

"Too late!" said Archie.

And then, in a flurry of flaps, the chickens came right at Bob. Quick as a flash, Bob used his super strength to flip a heavy wooden table on its side and leapt behind it. He spotted a sack of jewellery nearby and grabbed pawfuls of sparkly bangles and rings. Archie joined him and they started pelting the chickens with jewellery as they tried to fend off the advancing zombie army.

"Get the boogie blaster out!" Bob shouted to an invisible Archie as he lobbed a spangly tiara at one of the biggest zombie chickens. The chicken now had a diamond bracelet around his neck and his feathers were bedazzled with rubies and emeralds.

"It's over by the stairs," said Archie. "I put it down before we realised we were in a room full of zombie chickens!"

"Grab it, quickly!" said Bob. "I'm pretty sure if we get pecked by one of these little feathery monsters, we'll turn full zombie! The boogie blaster is our only hope!"

There was a gust of wind as invisible Archie whooshed across the room. As he rummaged through the bag, Bob could see things flying through the air as if by magic – a squashed cheese sandwich, a pair of sunglasses, a torch that would have been really handy five minutes previously...

But then Bob noticed something else.

"Archie! I can see your ears!" he shouted. "Your invisibility is wearing off!"

And Bob wasn't the only one who had noticed. One of the zombie chickens turned round just as Archie's furry bum was making an appearance.

"Archie! You need that boogie blaster NOW!" shouted Bob.

One by one, the other chickens noticed Archie and started slowly moving towards him. But just as Bob thought all was lost, Archie pulled out the boogie blaster!

"Found it!" said Archie, his paws trembling as he aimed at the chickens.

He took a deep breath, and then...

ZAAPPPP!!

The chickens froze mid-peck. Bob and Archie held their breath.

And then slowly, one by one, the chickens started to break out some

**SERIOUS MOVES.**

Zombie chicken number one was getting into classical ballet.

Chickens numbers two and three were disco dancing, while number four was spinning on its head.

And chicken number five was doing a tango with itself.

“It’s working!” shouted Bob, a bead of sweat dripping from his brow.

“Thank goodness!” said Archie. “Can we get out of here now? Who knows if there are more of them!”

But before they could head up the stairs, the door to the basement opened.

Bob and Archie exchanged a panicked look, then they hastily ducked back behind the upturned table.

Bob spotted the two bouncer armadillos. They were wearing protective suits and carrying a crate. Bob and Archie tried to stay as still as possible.

"Holy moly! The zombie chickens have escaped!" said the first armadillo. "And I'm pretty sure they weren't having a dance-off when we left them."

"How weird," said the other one. "Dr Colossus didn't mention that boogying was part of the zombie mutant process. Let's hope it's just these five and not the other five hundred!"

Bob and Archie gasped quietly.

**FIVE HUNDRED ZOMBIE CHICKENS!**

"Cluck, cluck! Come on, zombie chickens! You've got a job to do!" said the second armadillo, placing the crate on the floor.

He threw some seed into the crate and the zombie chickens all did the conga straight into it. Then the armadillos picked up the crate and headed up the stairs.

"We need to get away from this place as soon as possible!" said Archie.

"What are you talking about?" said Bob. "Didn't you hear the bit about Dr Colossus having an army of five hundred zombie chickens? We need to find out what he's up to."

“We had enough trouble with five zombie chickens,” said Archie. “I really don’t want to meet five hundred of them.”

“We can handle it!” said Bob. “We’re Koalas in Capes!”

“I’m really not sure we can,” said Archie, who was now pacing around the basement like a zombie chicken on fast forward. He was so stressed he managed to stub his toe on something resting up against the wall. It looked like a large painting with a sheet over it.

“Flaming furballs! My toe!” said Archie, kicking the painting in frustration. This not only made his toe hurt more, but also made the sheet fall away to reveal exactly what Dr Colossus was planning to do with five hundred and five zombie chickens...

# CHAPTER 12

## The Zombo-Copter 3000

UNDER THE SHEET was a detailed drawing of a very strange-looking helicopter.

"It's a blueprint!" said Archie.

"Looks like a helicopter to me," said Bob.

Archie rolled his eyes. "A blueprint is a design for something before you build it."

"But it's not even blue!" said Bob.

"It doesn't matter what colour it is!" said Archie. "That's the least of our problems."

Bob and Archie moved closer to take a look.

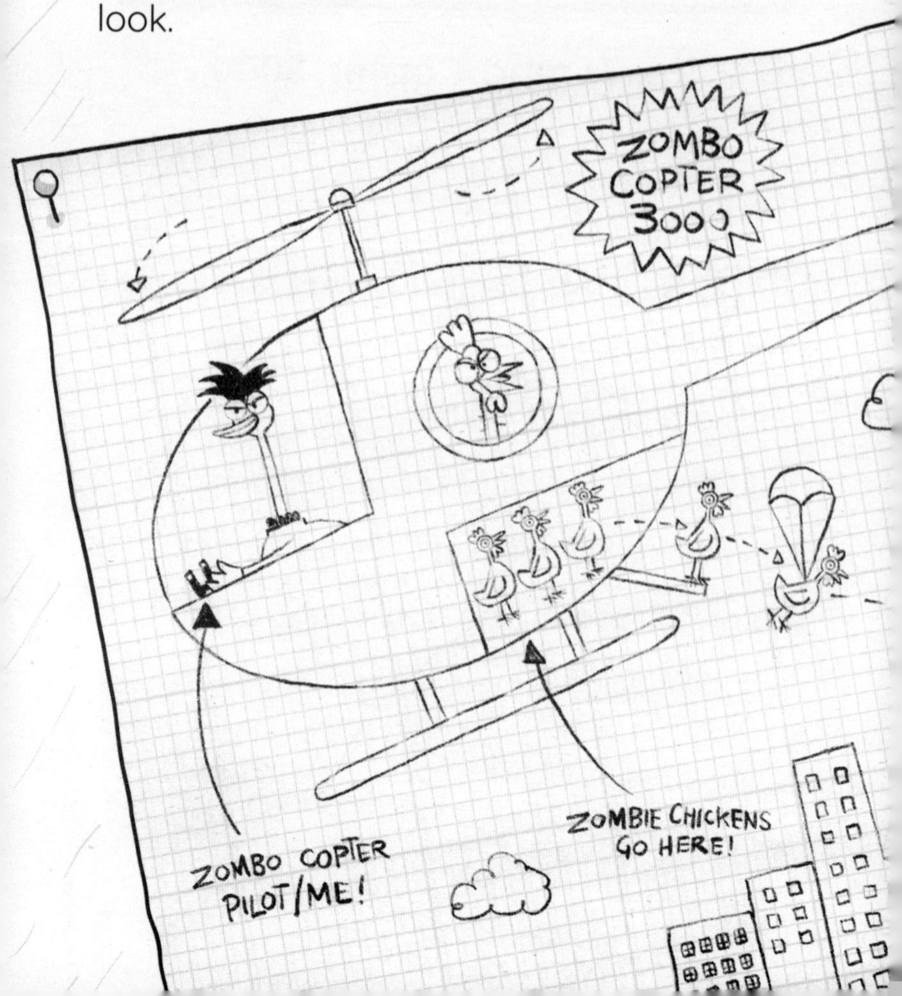

KITCHEN
BALLROOM
LIFT
HALLWAY
H
BIG BIRD MANSION LAYOUT
ONE PECK AND YOU'RE TOAST!
Mini trifles ✓
Cocktail cherries ✓
Party bags X
TO DO:-
BE EVIL!

Archie gasped. "Dr Colossus has made a

ZOMBO-COPTER!

And it's capable of releasing zombie chickens all over Pawtonia!"

"We've got to find that Zombo-Copter!" said Bob.

"Maybe it's on the rooftop?" said Archie.

"Good thinking!" said Bob. "We can just fly up there!"

"But what if the security guards spot us?" said Archie. "Surely there's another way to get to the roof?"

“There’s a lift over here,” said Bob, pointing to the map on the board. “We can get to it through the ballroom.”

“Wait!” said Archie. “Isn’t that the ballroom where all the supervillains are? That sounds

VERY DANGEROUS!

I really think it’s time we called in the kangatroopers!”

“There’s no time,” said Bob. “Dr Colossus could be jumping in that Zombo-Copter at any moment! Now, let’s get to the roof!”

Archie sighed. “I really wish saving

Pawtonia didn't have to be quite so dangerous," he said, reluctantly following Bob back up the stairs.

Bob and Archie headed down the corridor. They could see the door to the ballroom in front of them. Behind it, they could hear the clinking of glasses and the laughter of

EVIL SUPERVILLAINS.

Archie gulped. "If we really have to head through a ballroom full of supervillains, we should get rid of these waiter jackets," he said. "Last thing we want is to be slowed down by someone asking us for drinks or a fancy snack. It's better if they think we're guests."

"Good call," said Bob, and they quickly took off their jackets and shoved them in the coat rack. Then they headed into the ballroom where glamorous supervillains were milling around and a tuxedo-wearing band called Flamingo Royale were playing light jazz tunes on a stage.

"Hello, sirs, can I interest you in a villainous vol-au-vent or a curried egg?" said a gazelle waiter with a tray of delicious-looking canapés.

"Ooh, yes, please!" said Bob, taking a handful of both.

"Bob!" whispered Archie, giving him a nudge. "We're on a mission here; we haven't got time for nibbles!"

"But I'm starving, and they're delicious!" said Bob, spraying curried egg everywhere. "And we're meant to be supervillains having a good time!"

"I think you're having too much of a good time," said Archie. "Can you stop scoffing canapés and help me find the lift?"

"I can see it from here!" said Bob. "We just need to make our way over to the other side of the ballroom. Casually."

But just as they turned towards the lift, Bob felt a paw on his shoulder.

"I thought it was you!" said a large anteater with a cocktail clutched in one paw as he squeezed Bob's shoulder with the other.

Bob gulped and smiled nervously.

"I've only ever seen your pictures in Supervillains' Quarterly!" said the anteater. "It's an absolute honour to meet you both!"

Bob's paws felt clammy. They had clearly been mistaken for some super-villainous koalas.

"It's Frenzy and Chunk, isn't it?" said the

anteater, excitedly.

Bob gulped. Archie looked like he'd seen a ghost.

Bob knew what he had to do. There was only one thing for it...

"Yep, that's us!" he said, shaking the anteater's paw enthusiastically. "As supervillain koalas we can't resist a supervillain ball!"

And that's when Bob and Archie knew they were seriously

OUT OF THEIR DEPTH.

# ★ CHAPTER 13 ★

## The Wrong Koalas

"I'm a huge fan of your work!" said the anteater. "Can't believe you guys stole the world's most valuable diamond necklace from Prince Long Neck at the Royal Giraffe Jubilee – WHILE he was wearing it. Legendary!"

"Very kind of you," said Bob. "Would you

excuse us, we're actually just leaving. Flying visit!"

But the anteater wasn't listening.

"Melinda! Brett!" he shouted, waving over a pair of zebras. "Come and meet two of the

VERY BEST SUPERVILLAINS

in the business!"

Melinda and Brett trotted over excitedly.

"Great to meet you both," said Bob, as everyone shook hooves and paws.

Archie just stood completely still with a

crazed grin on his face.

The zebras looked totally starstruck.

"FRENZY AND CHUNK! THE KOALAS OF CARNAGE!"

said Melinda. "Word on the supervillain street is that you never make public appearances!"

"Well, we're just suckers for a curried egg, really," said Bob. "Isn't that right, Frenzy?"

Archie nodded, still grinning weirdly.

"Brett and I are just starting out as supervillains," said Melinda. "Mostly focusing

on heists and occasional animal-nappings, but we'd love your tips on becoming notorious! Any good stories?"

Bob gulped. Whoever these Koalas of Carnage were, they were clearly a huge deal.

"Well, stealing all that gold bullion was ridiculously dangerous and also thrilling!" said Bob. "At one point I was suspended from the ceiling deactivating the laser beam alarm system while Frenzy was holding off a whole mob of security guards who were trying to call the police..."

Everyone looked at Frenzy (aka Archie),

who was now nibbling at a curried egg, his paws ever so slightly shaking.

"Interesting," said the anteater. "I don't remember reading about that in the Supervillains' Quarterly feature piece."

"Well, of course they don't mention everything!" said Bob. "But that's definitely what happened! We should know – we are the

KOALAS OF CARNAGE,

after all!"

Archie jabbed Bob in the ribs. "Erm,

shouldn't we be getting on our way? We've got that ... thing to go to."

"Yes!" said Bob. "We do have that thing!"

"What a shame!" said the anteater. "But we understand, of course! Lovely to meet you!"

Bob and Archie could almost breathe again, but just as they were about to make their escape, the anteater piped up once more.

"Oh, wait, there's our host!" he said, waving at someone across the crowded ballroom. "You must say hello before you go."

The anteater called out, his voice cutting

through the noise of the ball, and a long feathery neck popped up above the crowd.

# CHAPTER 14

## There's a Feather in my Trifle!

**BOB AND ARCHIE** stood frozen in terror as Dr Colossus pushed his way through the crowd towards them, bowling over a small cluster of gentoo penguins on the way.

"Come and see who it is!" shouted the anteater, waving him over. "Your pals Frenzy and Chunk are here!

# "THE KOALAS OF CARNAGE!"

"Well, ruffle my villainous feathers," said Dr Colossus. The enormous ostrich bent his neck down to koala height and eyeballed Bob and Archie. "Welcome to the ball, Koalas of Carnage!"

But when he said "Koalas of Carnage" he said it really slowly and raised his big feathery eyebrows.

"Yup, that's us! Great to be here!" said Bob. "We love a supervillain ball, don't we?" Bob nudged Archie, who was still holding on to his curried egg with trembling paws.

"Interesting," said Dr Colossus, tapping one of his big clawed toes on the ballroom floor.

"Is it?" said Bob, suddenly panicking a bit. "Erm, everyone likes a ball, don't they?"

"Well, that's why it's interesting. Because Frenzy and Chunk hate parties. They always RSVP with a

**BIG FAT NO."**

"Oh, did I say we love parties? I meant we LOATHE them!" said Bob. "Look at Frenzy, he hates them so much he looks like he's got some kind of serious illness! And if that flamingo jazz band plays "Fly Me to the Moon" one more time, I'm going to..."

(Bob tried to think of what an evil supervillain might do when they didn't like something.)

"... tell them that everyone hates jazz music while Frenzy throws profiteroles at them!" said Bob.

But Dr Colossus was still tapping his big clawed toe and squinting at Bob and Archie like they smelled a bit funny.

"The thing is, boys," said Dr Colossus, "I just don't believe you. You don't have much of a

SUPERVILLAIN VIBE.

In fact, I'm not convinced you could hurt a fly."

Bob gulped. It was true. He had a soft spot for flies and often moved snails out of danger when he spotted them in high-traffic areas.

"But most importantly," continued Dr Colossus, "I've just been chatting to Frenzy and Chunk ...

and they're in New York on a doughnut factory heist."

Everyone in the group

**GASPED.**

Bob gulped and Archie went as white as a ghost.

Dr Colossus looked over to two of the security armadillos and gave them a nod.

"RUUUUN!" shouted Bob, grabbing an armful of mini trifles from the table and throwing them in the path of Dr Colossus.

SPLOOOOODGE!

SPLAT!

Archie shoved over a tower of profiteroles and they ran full pelt towards the exit.

SQUEEELCH!

Dr Colossus slipped and was soon flapping around in a pool of cream and chocolate like a massive ostrich trifle.

“Get those imposters!” shouted Dr Colossus. And the two armadillo bouncers rushed after Bob and Archie.

Bob and Archie ran past the jazz band and headed for the exit. Flamingo Royale were still playing despite the full-blown chase going on under their beaks. The armadillos were catching up.

“We need to slow them down!” said Archie.

“I’m on it!” said Bob, using his

**SUPER STRENGTH**

to pick up the grand piano and drop it in

front of the door to block the way. Bob and Archie slid underneath the piano on their furry bottoms and escaped through the door.

"Phew, that was close!" said Bob as they sprinted down a corridor. "We'll have to fly up to the rooftop. Quick, let's change into our capes!"

But opening the door to the outside, they ran straight into the armoured bodies of the two armadillos.

"Leaving so soon?" said one of them. "One minute you're desperate to get into the ball and the next you can't wait to leave."

"Yeah, you need to make your minds up!" said the other armadillo.

"We've got them!" said the first armadillo into an earpiece. "We'll bring them up to the rooftop, boss."

"Look, I'm sure we can work this out," said Bob, as he and Archie backed away before coming slap bang up against the mansion wall. "We were only here for the canapés and now we could do with a nap, so we'll just be on our way."

"I don't think so," said the armadillo. "The boss wants a word with you."

But as the two armadillos closed in on the koalas, Bob noticed one of them was carrying a big net. He raised his paw.

"OK, I've tried to be friendly," said Bob. "But if you won't play nice, then I must remind you that I have

**SUPER STRENGTH**

and I can throw you both over that fence like rugby balls."

But the armadillos just laughed and flung

the net over Bob and Archie.

"Let me show you what I think of this flimsy net!" said Bob.

However, when Bob tried to break free using his super strength, the ropes wouldn't give.

The armadillos chuckled.

"It's made from super-durable, titanium-infused rope," said the first armadillo.

"Just in case we happened to bump into any creatures with, you know, super strength," smirked the second armadillo. "We can never be too careful." He looked round. "Wait, where's the twitchy one?"

Bob hadn't noticed the disappearance of Archie either. He must have gone into invisible mode just before the net was thrown on them!

And as Bob heard the whoosh of a koala taking flight, he felt a glimmer of hope. This wasn't over yet! Maybe, just maybe, Archie could save the day...

# ★CHAPTER 15★

## The New Mayor of Pawtonia

**DR COLOSSUS** was standing on the rooftop of Big Bird Mansion surrounded by all of his supervillain guests. And Bob was right next to him locked up in a

TITANIUM CAGE.

From behind the bars, Bob had a perfect view of the

ZOMBO-COPTER 3000.

It looked much bigger than he had imagined from the drawing, and he could see the zombie chickens loaded in a big crate in the back. They were squawking and their eyes glowed red in the darkness. Bob rattled the bars of his cage, but they were way too strong even for his super strength.

"Ha ha!" said Dr Colossus. "So we've

nabbed ourselves a superhero koala! I've been expecting you! But I didn't think you'd be this easy to catch."

The armadillos patted themselves on their armoured backs, and the crowd of supervillains cheered.

"And it's only a matter of time before the rest of my security crew catch up with your little friend."

Bob put his head in his paws. There was still no sign of Archie. The city was in serious trouble and he was

COMPLETELY POWERLESS.

"And now for the

**GRAND FINALE!"**

said Dr Colossus, turning to his guests who were eagerly awaiting the

**BIG ANNOUNCEMENT.**

"Welcome, supervillains! Thank you for coming – we are just moments away from taking full control of Pawtonia!"

The supervillains whooped.

And the zombie chickens squawked.

"Oh yes, please don't get too close to the Zombo-Coptor," said Dr Colossus. "The zombie chickens are a bit temperamental so ensure you are out of pecking range at all times. We don't want any accidents!"

The crowd took a couple of paces back. And a nervous zebra ducked behind a large bin.

"We're about to broadcast live on every screen across the city!" boomed Dr Colossus. "Every billboard, every TV, every laptop and every smartphone will be showcasing my demand to become the Mayor of Pawtonia!"

Mandy, the lead robber duck, emerged from the Zombo-Copter wearing a chunky gold chain and a diamond tiara. She waddled over to a large camera and pressed some buttons.

"I'm ready!" shouted Dr Colossus.

"Action!" shouted Mandy, raising her wing.

And Dr Colossus began his speech.

"Good evening, creatures of Pawtonia! Some of you may already know me, but for those who don't – I am Dr Colossus, the most evil giant ostrich in the whole city! My ambition for world domination knows no bounds. So prepare to meet my demands

or face the consequences!"

At this point, Dr Colossus pointed a massive feathery wing at the camera.

"Make me the Mayor of Pawtonia, because if you don't ...

I WILL RELEASE ZOMBIE CHICKENS ACROSS THE CITY!

The Zombo-Copter 3000 is full of newly zombie-fied chickens. One peck and you're toast!

"Show them the zombie chickens, Mandy!" boomed Dr Colossus, and Mandy turned the camera towards the crate of super-gruesome red-eyed zombie chickens. They lurched at the camera and Mandy quickly panned back to Dr Colossus.

"People of Pawtonia, if you don't cooperate, the Zombo-Copter will be taking off and heading for the city centre. It's your choice!"

And then Dr Colossus did his evil cackle

with such gusto that he tripped over one of the camera cables and landed on his bum.

"Stop filming, Mandy! Don't film this bit!"

"Sorry, boss," said Mandy, turning off the live stream.

"You won't get away with this!" shouted Bob.

"I think you'll find that's exactly what I'm doing!" said Dr Colossus. "And no pesky koala is going to get in my way! I'm going to be the Mayor of Pawtonia and then I can do whatever I want!"

Mandy the robber duck waddled over to Dr Colossus clutching a mobile phone.

"What's the latest on our zombie ultimatum, Mandy?" said Dr Colossus. "Has the Mayor been in touch?"

"Erm, yes," said Mandy. "But I'm afraid they haven't agreed to your demands."

"What are you talking about?" said Dr Colossus. "Don't they know how dangerous I am? Fine. Let's see if they change their mind once I'm hovering over City Hall with a chopper full of zombie chickens! Start up the Zombo-Coptor!"

Another of the robber ducks jumped into the Zombo-Copter and there was a deafening thrum as its blades began to spin.

Dr Colossus climbed in and let out a long, raspy supervillainous laugh that seemed to go on for a good five minutes.

"MWAHAHA MWAHAHAHAHAHAHAHAH! MWAHAHAHAHAHAHAHAH AHAHAHHAAAAAAAAAA!"

Dr Colossus turned to Bob. "And there's no way that you and your little furry friend can save the day now!"

"I wouldn't be so sure about that!" said a voice. And Bob's heart soared, because he knew exactly who the voice belonged to...

# CHAPTER 16

## Operation Marshmallow

**BOB GRINNED** as he spotted a huge hot-air balloon rising up above the Big Bird Mansion rooftop. And not just any hot-air balloon – it was one promoting "THE BEST HOT STINKS IN TOWN!"

"Hi, Bob!" shouted Quinn through the loudhailer. "Need some help?"

TOWN

Archie was alongside her in the basket.

"Bob! We've come to save you!" shouted Archie, waving like he hadn't seen his friend for days.

Bob waved back excitedly. "Hi, guys! Thank goodness you're here!"

"I'm sorry to break up this heartfelt reunion," shouted Dr Colossus, "but I'm afraid your badly worded hot-air balloon is no match for my superior flying vessel. Good luck catching me when I'm in full flight!"

"Actually," shouted Quinn, "that's only the case if you're able to maintain aerodynamic propulsion when faced with a substance of high viscosity."

Dr Colossus looked confused (as did Bob and Archie). But as the Zombo-Copter started to rise up above the rooftop, all was revealed...

**"RELEASE THE MARSHMALLOWS!"**

shouted Quinn.

And with that, Archie and Quinn started tipping several large boxes of marshmallows over the side of the basket

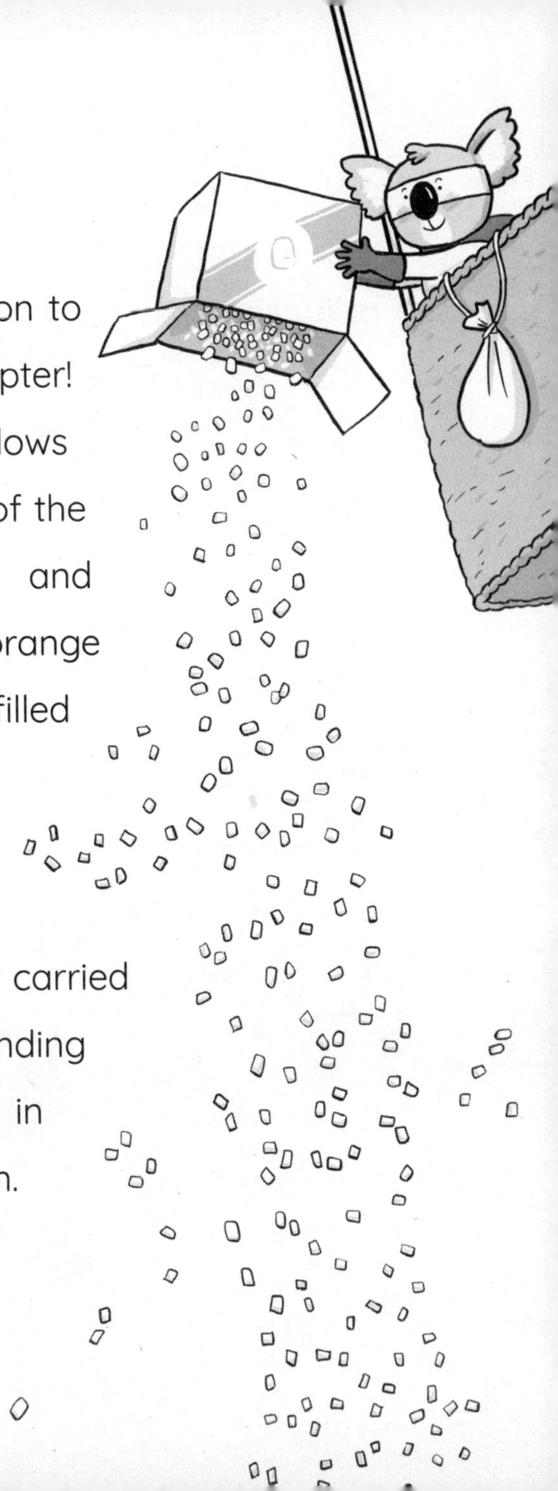

– and directly on to the Zombo-Copter! The marshmallows hit the blades of the Zombo-Copter and the smell of orange and caramel filled the air.

At first the blades of the Zombo-Copter carried on spinning, sending marshmallows in every direction.

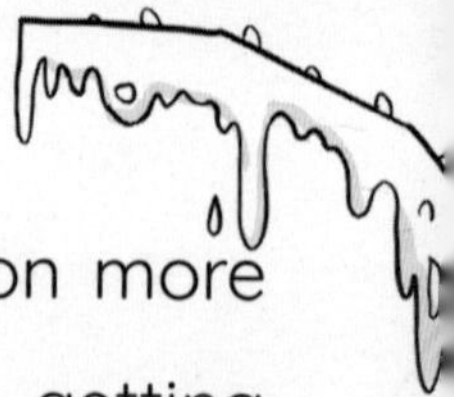

But as Archie and Quinn poured on more and more, the blades started getting clogged up.

Dr Colossus was furiously bashing the controls of the Zombo-Copter, but finally the blades ground to a halt. The Zombo-Copter nosedived back on to the rooftop with an almighty

The watching supervillains scattered. Fortunately, the zombie chickens remained safely in their crates, squawking loudly.

Meanwhile, Quinn was lowering the hot-air balloon on to the rooftop next to Bob, still locked up in his cage. One of the security guard armadillos was helping Dr Colossus get out of the badly damaged Zombo-Coptor.

"Archie, quick!" shouted Bob. "The keys to the cage are on the armadillo's belt loop!"

Archie looked extremely nervous and then he turned invisible. A gust of wind whooshed past Bob.

Bob watched as the keys magically floated off the armadillo's belt and headed in his direction.

"Look out!" shouted Bob, as the armadillo lunged for the keys. But invisible Archie threw them to Quinn, who quickly unlocked Bob's cage.

"Thanks, Quinn!" said Bob. "I can take things from here!"

Bob flew out of the cage and headed straight for the two armadillos. He picked them up, one in each paw, and flung them into the cage.

"That'll teach you to mess with Koalas in Capes!" said Bob.

And now it was time to finally capture Dr Colossus. But just as Bob was about to grab him, the giant ostrich pulled something out of his pocket.

"Look out, Bob!" said Archie, who had taken cover behind the hot-air balloon basket with Quinn. "He's got pondweed whumpers!"

Dr Colossus threw a whumper at Bob, but Bob quickly flew to safety and avoided the pondweed splurge. He took a breather next to the Zombo-Copter - nabbing a supervillain was hard work. But fortunately he wasn't on his own...

"Over here, you big feather pillow!" shouted Quinn.

"What did you call me?" said Dr Colossus. And as he turned away from Bob, Archie blasted him with the boogie blaster.

Within seconds, Dr Colossus was overcome by the irresistible urge to dance the macarena.

Bob swooped over to the enormous ostrich. They'd done it!

**KOALAS IN CAPES,**

with the help of Quinn, had captured their very first

**SUPERVILLAIN!**

But just as Bob was about to grab Dr

Colossus, the ostrich squawked.

"At least let me finish the moves!" said Dr Colossus. "If an ostrich is going to prison, he should be allowed to enjoy his last dance as a free bird."

This sounded fair to Bob. And anyway, he was tired and watching a giant ostrich do the macarena was pretty funny.

But then he heard Quinn shout, "The blaster's wearing off! He's tricking you! Grab him!"

Bob noticed Dr Colossus's dancing had got much worse. He wasn't under the influence of the blaster – these were his own rubbish moves! He was pretending!

By now, Dr Colossus had danced over to the edge of the rooftop where he was gyrating next to a large plastic capsule.

It was an escape pod!

Dr Colossus did one final boogie to the left, threw himself into the pod and fired himself into the night sky at full speed.

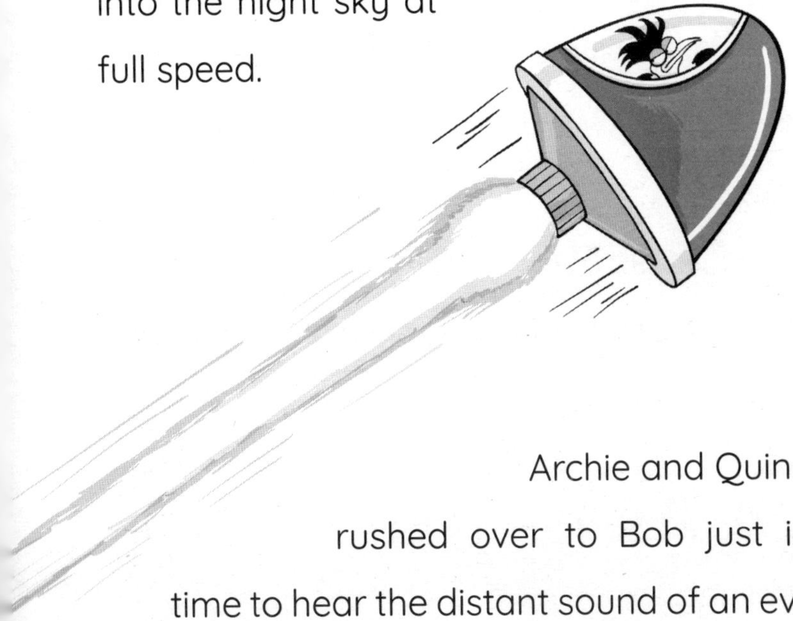

Archie and Quinn rushed over to Bob just in time to hear the distant sound of an evil ostrich squawking, "I'll be baaaaack!"

# CHAPTER 17

## Extremely Ruffled Feathers

**DR COLOSSUS** crash-landed on top of Mount Pointy on the outskirts of the city. This was unfortunate, because if he'd been slightly further west he would have crashed on Mount Squidgy and had a much softer landing.

Dr Colossus dusted off his feathers and

patted down his feathery eyebrows, which were a little bit on fire from the crash. This felt like a minor setback to Dr Colossus – he would take a short break and then come up with a

NEW AND IMPROVED PLAN

to take over Pawtonia. And next time he'd definitely get the better of those pesky koalas and their aardvark friend.

Nobody makes an evil giant ostrich look silly and gets away with it!

# ★CHAPTER 18★

## Hot Chocolate of Glory

**BOB, ARCHIE AND QUINN** squeezed into a booth at the back of the Hot Chocolate Café. Quinn's mum was making them extra-special hot chocolates to say well done for finishing their completely made-up project on Egyptian scarab beetles.

"I don't know what we would have done without you, Quinn," said Bob. "And your boogie blaster invention got us out of a tight situation ... twice! You're a

**TOTAL LEGEND!"**

"Strictly speaking, to be a legend I'd have to already be very famous and admired," said Quinn. But then she smiled. "Although I guess it's fair to say it was pretty cool."

Archie, on the other paw, didn't look happy at all.

"I feel really bad about lying," he said, as

Quinn's mum waved at them from behind the counter. She was adding marshmallows to three of the biggest hot chocolates ever created.

"I know," said Bob. "But I bet Quinn's mum would be making us even bigger hot chocolates if she knew we'd thwarted a

ZOMBIE APOCALYPSE!"

"She totally would," said Quinn. "And it's not our fault we can't tell anyone about

KOALAS IN CAPES.

The city depends on us, and if your true identities got out it would jeopardise everything."

Archie nodded in agreement, and a smile finally spread across his face.

Quinn's mum walked over with a tray laden with bumper-deluxe hot chocolates with all the toppings.

"Here you go, my little superstars!" said Quinn's mum. "I'm so proud of all the time you've put into that school project! Sounds like it was really boring!"

She gave the three of them a pat on the head, plus an extra squeeze of

Quinn's shoulder.

"Thanks, Mrs Burrows!" said Bob. "I've never done anything more BORING in my life!"

"Sooo boring!" said Archie, as all three of them tried desperately not to giggle.

The café doorbell tinkled as a busload of tourist otters piled in to escape the rain.

"I'd better go and deal with these soggy otters!" said Quinn's mum.

Now that they were on their own, Bob raised his hot chocolate mug. "Here's to

KOALAS IN CAPES,"

he said quietly. "We might not have caught Dr Colossus, but we did save the city from a major zombie chicken situation."

"Did you see the kangatroopers' faces when they realised we'd saved the day?"

said Archie, grinning. "Bet they'll be taking us more seriously from now on!"

Bob, Archie and Quinn clinked their mugs and basked in the awesomeness of a job well done.

Bob leaned back and took a long sip of his drink. "I think this might be my new favourite flavour."

"I don't think it's actually a flavour," said Quinn. "When it's a special occasion, Mum just puts everything in one big mug. It doesn't really have a name."

"It's got a name now," said Bob, holding his mug up like a trophy.

"THE HOT CHOCOLATE OF GLORY!"

Archie and Quinn whooped. And three friends with hot chocolate moustaches looked out the café window where the kangaroo steel drum band were playing in the city square once more. The rain had stopped, and a family of wombats had gathered round to listen to the music. All was well again in Pawtonia.

For now...

## ZOMBIE CHICKEN FOOTNOTE

All five hundred and five zombie chickens were successfully given a zombie antidote and made a full recovery. After their ordeal they were able to live their lives as ordinary chickens without bits dropping off them.